Dear Parent:
Your child's love of reading

Every child learns to read in a different way and at his or her own speed. Some go back and forth between reading levels and read favorite books again and again. Others read through each level in order. You can help your young reader improve and become more confident by encouraging his or her own interests and abilities. From books your child reads with you to the first books he or she reads alone, there are I Can Read Books for every stage of reading:

SHARED READING
Basic language, word repetition, and whimsical illustrations, ideal for sharing with your emergent reader

BEGINNING READING
Short sentences, familiar words, and simple concepts for children eager to read on their own

READING WITH HELP
Engaging stories, longer sentences, and language play for developing readers

READING ALONE
Complex plots, challenging vocabulary, and high-interest topics for the independent reader

ADVANCED READING
Short paragraphs, chapters, and exciting themes for the perfect bridge to chapter books

I Can Read Books have introduced children to the joy of reading since 1957. Featuring award-winning authors and illustrators and a fabulous cast of beloved characters, I Can Read Books set the standard for beginning readers.

A lifetime of discovery begins with the magical words "I Can Read!"

Visit www.icanread.com for information
on enriching your child's reading experience.

For Erin and Kate, who loved riding in their grandpa's old truck
and in our own red truck . . . they always wanted to go faster!—J.D.R.

For Grandpa Roger, the speed demon—B.D.

Adobe Illustrator™ was used to prepare the full-color art.

I Can Read Book® is a trademark of HarperCollins Publishers.

Axel the Truck: Speed Track. Copyright © 2013, 2018 by HarperCollins Publishers. All rights reserved. No part of this book may be used or reproduced in any manner whatsoever without written permission except in the case of brief quotations embodied in critical articles and reviews. Manufactured in China. For information address HarperCollins Children's Books, a division of HarperCollins Publishers, 195 Broadway, New York, NY 10007.

www.icanread.com

Library of Congress Control Number: 2018944018

ISBN 978-0-06-269279-5 (hardback)—ISBN 978-0-06-269278-8 (pbk. ed.)

18 19 20 21 22 SCP 10 9 8 7 6 5 4 3 2 1 First Edition

 Greenwillow Books

I Can Read!™

SHARED My First READING

Axel

THE TRUCK

Speed Track

Story by **J. D. Riley**

Pictures by **Brandon Dorman**

Greenwillow Books, *An Imprint of* HarperCollins*Publishers*

Axel is a red truck.

Axel has big, big wheels.

"Today is race day," Axel says.

Axel's big tires spin fast.

Zip, zip, zoom!

Axel's pal Rex rides along.

"Yahoo!" Axel yells.

"Arooo," Rex howls.

Axel heads for the fair.

The truck race is there.

The racetrack is loud.

There are tractors.

Chugga, chugga, chugga.

There are hot rods.

Roar, roar, roar!

Axel finds the trucks.

Vroom, vroom, varoom!

The trucks bounce their tires.

Thump, thump, thump!

The trucks are ready to roll.

Axel is number five.

His engine roars.

Vroom, vroom, varoom!

The starter lifts the flag.
Get ready! Get set! Go!

The speed is super fast.

Rex howls at the trucks they pass.
Axel is in third place!

Zip, zip, zoom!

Axel is in second place!

Go, Axel, go!

Axel's big tires spin faster.

Axel is in first place!
"Yahoo!" Axel yells.

Axel wins!

"Arooo!" Rex howls.

The trucks blast their horns.

Honk, honk, beep, beep!

Axel waves a big blue ribbon.

Vroom, varoom!

That was monster fun.